INTRODUCTION

Had I not pursued a career as an actress, I would have been a historian. Don't get me wrong, I have been on *Emmerdale* for the past thirteen years and I can honestly say I have loved every minute. It has given me an eye for how to create drama and excitement through interesting plots and diverse characters. But I think it is always important to put your energies into something you are passionate about, and writing children's history books allows me to combine both of my loves: to weave the drama of history with the enchantment of classic storytelling.

And so Princess Phoebe was born. But while

Phoebe may be a princess, she still has a lot to learn before she becomes Queen. Luckily, with the assistance of her mother's magical time travelling book, she has the help of all the interesting and crazy characters that history has to offer. The friends she meets along her way through time help her learn life's lessons and prepare her for the wider world.

I have always worried that young females are brought up on a rich diet of fairy-tale princesses whose single destiny seems to be that of meeting a handsome prince and living happily ever after. How lovely it has been to have the opportunity to present females whose strong and self-sustaining characters changed the course of history and whose lives are tales of strength, moral fortitude and overcoming life's obstacles (apart from those who were beheaded of course!).

I want Princess Phoebe and her tales to shake off the mustiness and fustiness of tired old history books. My reading matter largely consists of historical novels, books which combine historical accuracy with poetic licence to make dates and events come alive. This is what I have tried to emulate. I really want to fire the imagination. The most magical part of this process has been reading the finished product to my daughter, Mia. She adores history just as much as I do and it has been nothing short of wonderful for us to sit and enjoy these tales together. I hope you enjoy Princess Phoebe's exciting journey just as much as we do.

Sammy

CHAPTER ONE

Princess Phoebe lived in a big castle with her mum, Queen Alice, her dad, King George, and her little brother, Prince Peter.

The castle had hundreds and hundreds of rooms, all filled with glittering chandeliers, sofas bigger than beds and, best of all, lots of Queen Alice's sparkly dresses.

Like every little princess, Phoebe couldn't wait to grow up.

Every day after school, Phoebe raced home to try on her mum's pretty party gowns and tiaras. But there were such a lot. Phoebe wondered if she would ever have time to wear them all.

'Your mum never finds time either,' King George told Phoebe. 'But she still says she has nothing to wear!'

Phoebe's favourite room was Queen Alice's shoe and bag closet – chock full of beautiful handbags and glittery high-heeled shoes – even though no matter which pair Phoebe tried on, she always fell over.

'I'll never be a good queen if I can't walk in high heels,' moaned Phoebe one day.

'Being a queen is about more than walking in high heels and wearing pretty dresses, Phoebe,' said Queen Alice with a smile. 'Being a queen is about being brave and kind.'

But Phoebe wasn't listening, so Queen Alice left her daughter to play with the bags, shoes and beautiful jewellery.

Let loose, Phoebe had a brilliant time. And hours later, there were more of Queen Alice's clothes and jewellery on the floor than in the wardrobes.

What a mess!

'Oh no,' cried Phoebe. 'I'll never get this lot cleaned up before supper.'

Quickly Phoebe began stuffing her mum's clothes back into all the drawers and closets. But there was so much folding, cleaning and tidying to do that Phoebe soon felt very tired and sat on a pile of dresses for a little rest.

Just as Phoebe was about to shut her eyes and enjoy a nap, a big gold photo album lying underneath a box of bracelets caught her eye.

Phoebe had never seen the album before and curiously started flipping through the pages. She squealed with glee. There were lots of family pictures of princesses and queens. They were all so beautiful, apart from one or two. For example, there was a Princess Paula, who had a wonky nose, Lady Louise with cauliflower ears and Dame Dolly, who had a huge wart on both cheeks.

All too soon, Phoebe reached the end of the album, and just as she turned to the last page, she saw a drawing of a beautiful looking princess named Anne Boleyn, wearing a pretty black dress, studded with jewels.

Staring hard at the picture, Phoebe didn't think she'd ever seen such a glamorous dress. Then, without warning, the picture started to move.

First it juddered to the left. Then to the right, and suddenly Anne Boleyn's hand had come to life as it reached out from the photo towards Phoebe.

'I'm glad you've come along,' said Anne. 'I've

been really bored standing in this picture waiting for someone to talk to.'

By now Phoebe's eyes were out on stalks.

'You're a picture,' squeaked Phoebe. 'You can't speak.'

'I can and I am,' laughed Anne. 'Take my hand and I'll show you what my life was like as a princess.'

Phoebe thought quickly. Her mum and dad were always telling her not to run off with strangers.

But Anne wasn't a stranger.

She was her great, great, great, great, great something or other – well, she was family anyway!

Before she could change her mind, Phoebe grabbed Anne's hand.

Holding her breath, Phoebe felt a whoosh in her tummy as everything started spinning faster and faster like she was on a rollercoaster, until finally she couldn't see anything anymore.

CHAPTER TWO

Phoebe felt like she was hurtling through the air at a million miles an hour. Then all of a sudden everything came into focus and she landed next to Anne with a loud thud.

'Ooof!' grumbled Anne. 'No wonder you can't walk in high heels if you're always so heavy on your feet.'

But Phoebe was too busy looking around to take any notice. There were so many lush green fields and trees – it was like being in a forest.

'Where are we?' she asked.

'Norfolk,' Anne replied. 'Can you see that building

over there?'

Squinting her eyes against the midday sun, Phoebe could see a huge, red-brick palace complete with a turret in the middle.

'It's beautiful,' Phoebe said.

'I was born there in 1501,' replied Anne.

'You're ancient!'

'Thanks a lot. I got bullied enough without you joining in.'

'But you're a princess,' chimed Phoebe. 'Princesses can't get bullied.'

'Everyone can get bullied, Phoebe,' Anne said. 'Rich, old, young, poor, and it's always mean!'

Anne wiped tears from her eyes, before explaining that when she was a young girl people made up lots of nasty stories about her.

'They said I was ugly and had six fingers on my hand.'

'How horrible,' gasped Phoebe.

'I got my own back by growing up into a beautiful queen,' said Anne with a grin. 'I was praised for my long neck, which was brilliant for showing off nice dresses. Look.'

Suddenly Phoebe's tummy went all whooshy again. She closed her eyes and when she opened them they were in a huge room filled with clothes. Phoebe's eyes were as wide as saucers as she took in all the glittery dresses. There were rails and rails of frocks. Anne had even more clothes than her mum!

But before Phoebe could try on even a single one, she heard voices in the corridor.

'Bonjour, Mademoiselle.'

'Who's that?'
asked Phoebe.
'A servant,'
whispered Anne.

'But why is he speaking French?'

'Because we're in my bedroom in France.'

'France!' shrieked Phoebe. 'How did we get to France?'

Just like Phoebe's mum, Anne ignored her, and instead, she moved to the window and waved down a man standing below.

'Why are you waving to that man?' asked Phoebe.

'You ask a lot of questions,' Anne chided. 'If you must know, I'm waving because that's the French King, Louis XII. Henry VIII's sister Mary Tudor married him and I worked for them.'

'Cool,' said Phoebe. 'Did you stay here long?'

But just as Phoebe asked the question, the room started spinning again.

CHAPTER THREE

'Before you ask, we're at Hampton Court,' Anne said, as they landed next to a magnificent red brick palace. 'This was Henry VIII's favourite palace and I lived here with my sister, Mary. A couple of years later we both worked here for his wife, Catherine of Aragon.'

As Anne took Phoebe on a guided tour of Henry's Royal Court, Phoebe was excited to see a real ball taking place. It was full of very grand men and women dancing.

'We had banquets and balls,' said Anne. 'And only rich ladies were allowed to wear bright colours. Plus if

the King or Queen walked past, then you had to curtsey until they had gone, and you were never, ever allowed to turn your back on them.'

'That sounds like a lot to remember,' said Phoebe.

'Only if you're a fopdoodle,' said Anne, laughing.

'A fop what?' replied a rather puzzled Phoebe.

'What are they teaching princesses these days?' Anne sniffed. 'Fopdoodle means idiot, nincompoop, fool, and you obviously are one if you don't know what that means!'

'Am not!' cried Phoebe.

'Are too!' shot back Anne.

'Am not!'

'Oh this is getting us nowhere! Do you want to hear how Henry and I became friends or not?' Anne asked.

Phoebe sulkily shrugged her shoulders, even though secretly she couldn't wait to hear the rest of Anne's story.

'Well, Henry showered my family and me with gifts and royal titles,' Anne continued. 'He wrote me letter after letter. We fell head over heels in love and wanted to marry.'

'Wait a minute,' interrupted Phoebe. 'You said Henry was already married to Catherine of Aragon.'

'Yes, but that didn't stop Henry,' said Anne. She chuckled. 'He asked the Archbishop of Canterbury to annul his marriage to Catherine, which is a bit like a divorce.'

By now, Phoebe was so lost in the story she completely forgot how cross she was with Anne for calling her an idiot.

'What happened next?'
she begged.

Anne explained that
Henry's decision to
remarry upset the
Catholic Church
so he started
his own – the

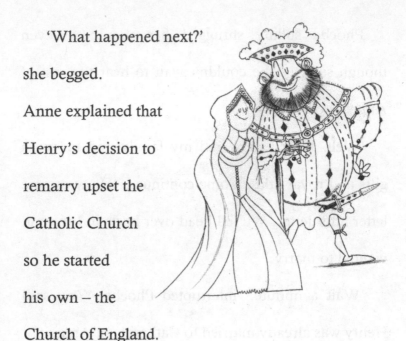

Church of England.

'We married at a secret ceremony in January 1533
in the King's private chapel.' Anne smiled. 'It was
really exciting and romantic, and when I was crowned
Queen all our friends and family celebrated with us at
a huge banquet.

'It sounds beautiful,' said Phoebe dreamily.

'It was,' agreed Anne. 'All the streets were

decorated with gold cloth, tissue and velvet, and I wore a gorgeous white dress and a gold coronet.'

'What happened next?' asked Phoebe, agog.

'Well, Henry and I were very happy and in love. Then I gave birth to our daughter, Elizabeth, in August 1533.' Anne smiled. 'She was gorgeous, with pale, porcelain skin and a shock of fiery bright red hair, just like her dad.'

'Sounds like you all lived happily ever after,' said Phoebe expectantly. 'I hope I marry someone like Henry.'

'I hope you don't!' snorted Anne. 'After Elizabeth was born, Henry turned into a monster.'

'What, a real one?' asked Phoebe, picturing Henry covered in green scales with bulging purple eyes.

'No!' replied Anne. 'He just turned into a big

meanie.'

Anne explained that Henry was disappointed Elizabeth was a girl because he wanted a son to take over the throne when he died. After all, his first wife, Catherine of Aragon, had been pregnant six times, but only one of those children survived – his daughter Mary.

'That was when he didn't want to be friends with me anymore and made friends with one of my ladies in waiting – Jane Seymour.'

'Wow,' breathed Phoebe. 'I can't wait to tell all my friends your story.'

'Are you always this much of a gossip?' asked Anne. 'You should be careful you don't find yourself in the brank.'

'Ooh, did you have many branks?' asked Phoebe.

'I love going to the one in the high street with my mum and dad and counting up all our gold.'

'Not a bank!' hissed Anne. 'A brank, an iron bridle that was put around the heads of women who gossiped too much!

'It's time to move on,' said Anne as she reached for the girl's hand. Phoebe felt that familiar whooshy feeling in her tummy as the room started to spin again.

CHAPTER FOUR

Phoebe and Anne appeared in a little grey room with a dirty blanket on the floor and a tiny cracked window. It was a far cry from the palaces and courts Phoebe had seen so far.

'This place looks like a prison,' Phoebe whined as she peeped through the window and saw an unfortunate man with a ball and chain, his head and wrists trapped in what Phoebe believed to be stocks, but in truth were actually called pillories.

'Prison, yes, that's exactly what it is,' said Anne. 'In 1536 Henry fell out of love with me and wanted to marry Jane, so he had me arrested and locked up in

this tiny room in the Tower of London.'

'What did you do?' Phoebe asked.

'Nothing,' Anne replied firmly. 'But that didn't stop Henry saying I was a witch who made up spells and even plotted to kill him.'

'Aaaagh!' shrieked Phoebe, leaping back from Anne. 'Don't turn me into a frog!'

'It wasn't true,' Anne protested. 'You really are a fopdoodle if you think that! But a court still found me guilty – they were all fopdoodles too!'

'What happened then?' begged Phoebe, sensing a nasty end to the story.

'I was taken outside to a scaffold. I was scared, but knew I had to say nice things about Henry as he was the king, so I told the small crowd he was good and noble. Then, I kneeled down and tried to ignore all the

people shouting "off with her head" and unlike my daughter's generation I didn't have to wait for Derrick.'

'Who's Derrick?' Phoebe said, by now genuinely confused.

'Derrick's the hangman!' snapped Anne. 'Blimey, are you sure you're a princess if you don't even know Derrick means hangman?'

'Er, we don't have a hangman anymore,' said Phoebe.

'Really?' gasped Anne.

'Yes, all that went out years ago – if princesses are naughty, we just get told off, or if we've been really bad, we have to go around to our great grandad Prince Paul's house and listen to him tell a lot of really rude jokes for hours.'

'Doesn't sound so bad,' said Anne, shrugging.

'You've obviously never met Great Grandad!' Phoebe replied.

By now, Phoebe didn't even notice the whooshy feeling in her tummy as they disappeared from the tiny prison room and reappeared in a church.

'We're in the chapel just outside the Tower of London,' said Anne. 'This is where my body was laid to rest after I was killed, and where other princesses, like you, can come and see me.'

Phoebe thought that was very sad. She reached out to give Anne's hand a squeeze, but just as she touched Anne's fingers, Phoebe saw a woman walk into the chapel.

'This is Jane Grey, a friend of mine,' said Anne. 'She was Queen for only nine days – I'd like you to spend some time with her.'

'Wh…what? Why?' stuttered Phoebe.

But Anne had already disappeared, leaving her alone with Jane.

Turning to face her new friend, Jane reached out and took Phoebe's hand and they began to fly.

'I've a lot to show you,' smiled Jane. 'Are you ready?'

CHAPTER FIVE

Climbing higher and higher, Phoebe wondered if they were going all the way to the moon!

Thankfully, lush green trees and fields came into focus as Jane expertly guided them to the ground.

'You're better at this than Anne,' Phoebe marvelled, delighted not to have another grass stain to explain to her mum.

'I've always been a quick learner,' said Jane, smiling. 'When I was your age, I loved learning languages and homework.'

Phoebe's eyes widened. She hated homework!

'Don't worry. You're not the only one who

thought I was mad because I enjoyed reading instead of playing outside with my friends,' said Jane, laughing. 'My mum and dad were really strict and always encouraged me to go out hunting or sew.'

'Oooh, I'm rubbish at sewing,' Phoebe muttered. 'I'm rubbish at riding horses too.'

'There's more to life than any of those things,' Jane assured the little girl. 'What's important is finding something you're good at and enjoy. I always tried telling my parents that but they never listened.'

'Who were your parents and why are we in the middle of nowhere?' Phoebe demanded as they walked towards a large medieval house surrounded by forest.

'Anne warned me you ask a lot of questions,' teased Jane. 'Perhaps if I start at the beginning, you might not ask so many! I was born in 1537, my mum was Lady Frances Brandon, Henry VIII's little sister, and my dad was Henry Grey, 1st Duke of Suffolk. The house in front of you is Wulfhall in Wiltshire.'

'Is this where you were born?' Phoebe asked, letting go of Jane's hand and wandering towards the house for a closer look.

'No. I was born in Leicestershire, and because Henry VIII was my uncle, I was sent to court to live with his sixth and final wife, Catherine Parr, when I was just nine years old.'

'Nine,' squeaked Phoebe. 'That's only a year older than me now.' Terrified at the thought of being sent away from her mum and dad, Phoebe returned to Jane's side and squeezed her hand.

'Weren't you scared?' she asked quietly.

Jane shook her head. 'No. I didn't really get on with Mum and Dad. Besides, Catherine was so welcoming and she showered me with love.'

'Sounds nice. Did Catherine let you play with all her dresses too?'

'I didn't want to dress up. I just wanted to read and learn Greek, Latin and Hebrew. Catherine helped me by making sure I had tutors and she also taught me to follow Henry VIII's Christian Protestant faith.'

'Sounds boring!' Phoebe protested.

'It's actually really interesting,' replied Jane. 'Look.'

'So no dresses at all then?' Phoebe asked sadly as Jane put her old schoolbooks away.

Jane roared with laughter. 'Is dressing up all you think about?'

'No!' snapped Phoebe crossly. 'I just think a Princess should look pretty, that's all.'

'You're right, Phoebe, and I did wear pretty dresses much later,' Jane soothed. 'But being pretty isn't everything. Being honest, courageous and loyal is far more important as a princess. Something I found out much later, after I got married at fifteen.'

'You got married at fifteen!' Phoebe marvelled. 'What happened?'

'All in good time,' said Jane, smiling as she wandered towards the house. 'Wulfhall belonged to Catherine. When Uncle Henry died in 1547, his younger son, Edward VI, became King. Catherine married Thomas Seymour and she moved here along with Henry's daughter, Elizabeth I, who Catherine promised to look after. I moved in with them.'

As Jane grabbed hold of Phoebe's hand, Phoebe felt that familiar whooshy feeling in her tummy.

CHAPTER SIX

Phoebe and Jane were standing in a long banqueting room filled with a wooden table, high-backed chairs and oak panelling. Heavy, red velvet drapes lined the windows, and the family coat of arms – a red shield with three gold lions and a pair of wings – decorated the back wall.

'Wow!' Phoebe breathed. 'This place is gorgeous.'

Jane said nothing as she walked towards the window and pointed to a garden filled with poppies and roses. 'Outside, Elizabeth and I would play together and read books. We were all very happy. Then when Catherine gave birth to a little girl we were

all delighted.'

'Awww, cute,' said Phoebe with a grin. 'I love babies.'

'So did Catherine,' replied Jane forlornly. 'Sadly she died a week later following complications after the birth and her little girl, Mary Seymour, went to live with one of her close friends.'

'What about you?' Phoebe asked, sensing Jane was very upset.

'I was very sad,' Jane admitted. 'I loved Catherine so much. I was chief mourner at her funeral and completely lost without her.'

'Afterwards Thomas became my guardian and looked after me for twelve months, but then he was arrested for embezzlement and beheaded in 1549. Then John Dudley, King Edward's chief advisor, became my guardian and in May 1553 he made me

marry his son, Lord Guildford Dudley.'

'So there was a happy ending after all,'

Phoebe squealed as she danced

excitedly around Jane.

'Was he a handsome prince?

Did he sweep you off

your feet and spoil

you for the rest of

your life, hand-feeding

you chocolates

and grapes?'

'I wish!' Jane snarled. 'I hated John Dudley! He was mean and nasty just like his son.'

Phoebe's eyes widened in alarm. 'Then why did you marry him?'

'I was made to! My parents were ambitious and so was John Dudley. He wanted Guildford to become King. Because I was Henry VIII's niece, he knew that if his son married me it was much more likely,' Jane insisted.

'That's horrible!' Phoebe protested. 'At least tell me you had a pretty wedding dress.'

'Huh!' huffed Jane. 'See for yourself.'

As Jane angrily grabbed Phoebe's hand, the two flew through the air at breakneck speed. Soon the trees and fields gave way to clusters of buildings and Phoebe realised they were back in London.

CHAPTER SEVEN

Landing inside a posh mansion, Phoebe took a minute to get her breath back and admire her surroundings. As she wandered through the huge house, she saw the place had a large chapel and high ceilings. There were more rooms overlooking the River Thames than Phoebe could count, and not just because her maths teacher had given her an F for her last piece of homework! It was because there were so many it would take her all day to count them up.

Returning to Jane's side, she saw her guide was standing on the edges of a grand hall supported by marble pillars. Phoebe could see there were tears in her eyes as she looked at the sea of noblemen and women all dressed up in their finery and dancing to the music. Phoebe felt very sorry for her. Jane seemed so nice.

'This was my wedding day,' Jane sniffed. 'It should have been the happiest day of my life. But it was horrible. Everything was so rushed; it wasn't just me that got married that day but my younger sister, Katherine, and Dudley's daughter Catherine too.'

'There are a lot of Catherine's in this story,' Phoebe pointed out. 'I'm having a lot of trouble keeping track.'

Despite her tears, Jane laughed. 'You're not the only one. But look, there I am now, can you see?'

As Phoebe craned her neck and followed where Jane was pointing, she saw just how miserable her

guide was. She may have been married but her tiny
freckled face was red from crying. To add insult to
injury, Jane's gown of
gold and silver brocade,
decorated with diamonds
and pearls, was far too
big, making her look
even thinner and
shorter than
she already was.

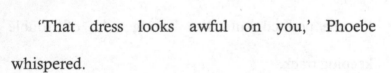

'That dress looks awful on you,' Phoebe
whispered.

'That's because it was borrowed from the Royal
Master of the Wardrobe the morning of my wedding.
I didn't even choose it,' Jane replied miserably.

'Well, if you had chosen it, I bet you'd have chosen

something a lot nicer,' said Phoebe loyally.

As Jane reached for her hand, Phoebe flashed her little smile. She felt bad for Jane. Nobody deserved to marry someone they didn't love and look bad at the same time. She was just about to say as much when the room started spinning and that strange whooshy sensation started again in Phoebe's tummy.

'This is Sion House,' Jane announced, as they landed in a very large, grand room. A huge wooden chair stood in the corner, thick heavy curtains surrounding it, while noblemen and women stood anxiously alongside.

'This is where I was told I was Queen,' Jane explained simply.

Phoebe looked at Jane in surprise. 'Wait a minute. You said Edward was King. Where's he gone?'

'Edward died,' Jane explained. 'He got measles, then tuberculosis and on his deathbed named me as successor to the throne.'

'Goodness!' breathed Phoebe. 'But what about Elizabeth? Wasn't she Henry's daughter and Edward's sister?'

'She was,' Jane agreed. 'And there was her older sister, Mary, too. But because Henry's marriages to Mary and Elizabeth's mums weren't considered legal, nobody thought they had a right to be Queen. Just in case though, John Dudley made Edward agree to make me heir before he passed away. He didn't want the throne falling back into the Catholic hands of Mary.'

'What a meanie,' Phoebe whispered. 'But weren't you excited to be Queen?'

'I was. But I didn't think I'd earned it. Mary was the rightful heir as Henry's eldest child.'

'Did you say anything?' Phoebe asked.

'I tried,' Jane said. 'But my parents were very strict and insisted. I was very religious and brought up to do what I was told but I refused to make Guildford King.'

'No! What did everyone say about that?' Phoebe gasped.

'They weren't happy about it,' Jane said with a chuckle. 'I rowed with everyone for days. But I hardly knew Guildford, so I made him the Duke of Clarence instead. I could hardly make him King of England, could I?'

'I suppose not,' Phoebe agreed. 'So what did you wear to your coronation?'

'I had a lovely dress in green and white, which

were the Tudor's signature colours, and because I'm quite short I had to wear a pair of raised wooden shoes called chopines to make me look taller.'

'Wood! For shoes? Yuck! How uncomfortable,' said Phoebe with a shudder.

'They were a bit,' Jane agreed. 'But I wasn't in them for long, as a barge took me and all my attendants along the river so I could be crowned Queen.'

Just as Phoebe was about to open her mouth, Jane reached for Phoebe's hand. 'I'll show you,' she said, whisking Phoebe high above the London skyline then bringing them gently back to earth.

'I know where this is,' Phoebe shouted triumphantly. 'This is the Tower of London, where Mummy keeps her jewels. Are we going inside?'

Jane shook her head. 'I promised myself I'd never go back inside that building. It holds too many bad memories.'

'Come on,' Phoebe encouraged. 'Didn't you tell me earlier a princess had to have courage?'

'That's different,' Jane said crossly.

'No it isn't,' replied Phoebe. 'You sound like my little brother, Peter, when Mummy won't let him have a pudding if he hasn't eaten all his vegetables. He always tells her it's a different kind of hunger but Mummy never gives in. You shouldn't either.'

This time, Phoebe slipped her hand into the bigger girl's and squeezed her fingers. 'What's the worst that could happen?' she asked.

'Oh alright,' Jane sighed.

Feeling Jane's fingers tighten around her palm,

Phoebe prepared herself for another whooshy sensation. But this time they were so quick, she barely noticed they'd left the ground.

CHAPTER EIGHT

'T his is the White Tower,' Jane explained. 'It's the central tower and oldest part of the castle.'

Phoebe looked around her. With its large onion-shaped dome, it was both beautiful and scary. 'Weren't you nervous?' the little girl wondered.

'A bit,' admitted Jane. 'It didn't help that when we travelled along the Thames in the barge the general public were all silent. They were shocked Edward had died and an unknown fifteen-year-old was taking his place.'

'How horrible,' Phoebe gulped. 'Everyone is

always so lovely to Mummy and Daddy. Mummy gets so many flowers she said she could open up her own florist's shop!'

'That sounds nice,' sniffed Jane. 'I didn't get any flowers.

But when I arrived at the Tower guns rang out in salute and the whole place was filled with silky flags in my honour.'

'That doesn't sound so bad,' Phoebe shrugged.

'It wasn't, I suppose,' Jane replied. 'I was made Queen in July 1553, four days after Edward died. A couple of days later there was a church service where everyone was encouraged to support me as their new monarch.'

'And did they?' Phoebe asked.

'Well, the trouble was Mary had now discovered her brother was dead and I'd been made Queen without her knowledge,' Jane said, flopping onto one of the pews in the tower's chapel.

'No!' protested Phoebe, as she joined Jane. 'You mean nobody told her?'

Jane shook her head. 'She was angry. She said she should be Queen and the people agreed with her.'

'Did she win?' Phoebe asked, afraid she already

knew the answer.

'She did.' Jane nodded. 'Nine days after I was crowned Queen of England, Mary was publicly named Queen and everybody had street parties they were so happy.

'It was a pretty horrible time,' Jane admitted. 'Mary kept me prisoner, accused me of stealing all her jewels and then sentenced me and Guildford to death in 1554, when I was just sixteen.'

Phoebe clamped her hands over her mouth. 'You poor thing.'

'I was so scared,' Jane continued. 'Guildford was beheaded at Tower Hill, then it was my turn. I was taken to Tower Green, where I handed my gloves and hankie to my maid and the executioner said he was really sorry about what he was going to do.'

'Was that Derrick?' Phoebe asked quietly, proud she'd remembered something Anne had taught her.

'No,' said Anne. 'He was the hangman, but well done for listening.'

Phoebe squirmed.

'The next thing I knew, it was all over. I was just sixteen, Phoebe!'

As Phoebe clasped her hands over Jane's to comfort her, she saw another woman, with flaming red hair, stride towards them.

'Telling your sob story again, are you, Jane?' she called.

'Who are you? And stop being horrible to my friend!' Phoebe shouted loyally.

'Oh be quiet, pipsqueak!' the woman snapped.

Instinctively Phoebe jumped away from the

woman and whispered in Jane's ear.

Jane lifted her head. 'This is Mary I. She's the one that had me killed!'

'Aaaagh!' Phoebe shouted as she swatted Mary with her hands. 'That was a very mean thing to do!

You shouldn't chop people's heads off! Not even if they've been very bad. You could have just put Jane on the naughty step for an hour. That's what Mummy does to me if I'm bad.'

'What are you talking about, girl?' Mary hissed. 'No, forget it. I don't want to know. Actually, I very nearly spared Jane's life.'

'Very nearly isn't the same as actually sparing though, is it?' Jane pointed out.

'No. But it's not my fault your dad joined a rebellion to have me taken from the throne.' Mary said. 'If he hadn't done that, I wouldn't have had your head chopped off.'

'Yes, you would,' Jane protested.

'No, I wouldn't,' Mary shouted.

By now Phoebe had her hands over her ears,

having heard quite enough. 'SHUT UP!' she yelled. 'Or I'll put you both on the naughty step. Now why can't you try to be friends?'

Jane turned and smiled at Phoebe. 'We are really. That whole beheading thing is in the past now, isn't it, Mary?'

'It is,' Mary agreed. 'Besides, I had my own problems. Want to see, Phoebe?'

As Mary held out her hand, Phoebe reluctantly took it. Something told her Mary's story would mean she was in for a very bumpy ride.

CHAPTER NINE

Phoebe's instincts weren't wrong. First her tummy gurgled to the left. Then it gurgled to the right. Then it gurgled up and down, so much she thought she was going to be sick! Glancing up at her guide, as she inexpertly guided them across the city, Phoebe spotted a no-nonsense look in her eye. Something told Phoebe that if Mary found out she was about to bring up her breakfast she'd be in trouble.

As they hit the ground, Phoebe was so grateful to still be in one piece that she didn't notice how close they were to the River Thames. Exhausted, she leant back, only for Mary to pull her to her feet.

'Foolish child!' she snapped. 'You nearly fell in the river.'

Dazed after the bumpy ride, Phoebe looked around her. Mary was right. One step back and she'd be in the murky water suffering a very different kind of tummy trouble.

'Sorry,' Phoebe said meekly. 'But if you didn't want us to fall in the water, why did we land so close to it?'

Mary glared at Phoebe. 'One can't be good at everything. And flying isn't my strong suit.'

'You can say that again,' Phoebe muttered cheekily.

Fortunately Mary didn't hear. She walked towards the giant palace. 'This is where I was born in 1516!' Mary announced in a booming voice.

'I know where we are. It's the old Naval College in Greenwich,' said Phoebe, joining Mary in front of the grand building. 'Grandad sometimes brings me and Peter here because he says it's important we look at architecture.'

'Your grandfather sounds a wise man,' Mary said primly.

'Yes he is… it's very pretty,' Phoebe said, walking closer to the palace built around three large courtyards.

'Pretty!' shrieked Mary. 'It's more than pretty – it's very important.'

'Why?' asked Phoebe.

'What do you mean why? Are you sure you're a princess if you don't even know your family's own history? Not only was I born here but I lived here very happily for many years, as did my sister, Elizabeth.'

'It's a nice place to grow up,' Phoebe agreed. 'My little brother and I always play chase in the park when we visit. What did you do here?'

'Play chase!' Mary gasped. 'Good gracious. Playing chase is not what a royal does.'

'It's fun though,' Phoebe replied. 'Didn't you have fun when you were little?'

Mary raised her eyes to the sky and muttered something under her breath which Phoebe didn't quite catch.

'I was a very gifted child, and unlike you whose sole ability appears to be playing chase, I had lots of talents and hobbies,' Mary said haughtily. 'When I was four I entertained the French with a performance on a harpsichord, and I was brilliant at Latin, Spanish, music, dance and Greek.'

'Anything you weren't good at?' Phoebe asked naughtily. She knew she shouldn't think badly of Mary, but so far Phoebe thought her new guide was a royal pain in the bum.

'Not really,' Mary replied. 'Daddy always described me as the greatest pearl in the kingdom.'

'Who was your daddy?' Phoebe asked politely.

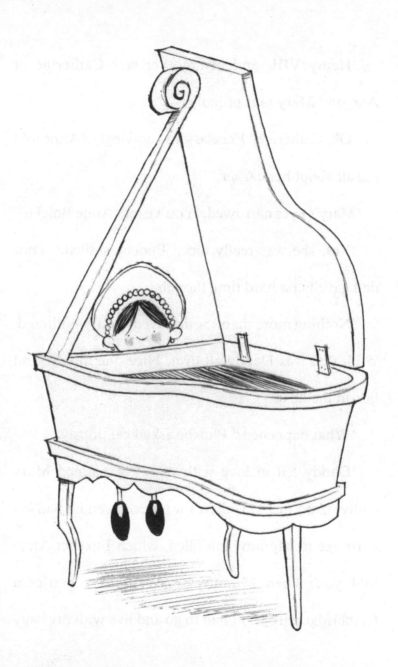

'Henry VIII, and my mother was Catherine of Aragon,' Mary said proudly.

'Oh, Catherine,' Phoebe said knowingly. 'Anne told me all about her earlier.'

Mary's eyes narrowed. 'You've met Anne Boleyn?'

'Yes, she was really nice,' Phoebe smiled. 'Your dad gave her a hard time though.'

'Nothing more than she deserved,' Mary muttered. 'Still, that was Daddy all over. Nice one minute and horrid the next.'

'What happened?' Phoebe asked cautiously.

'Daddy fell in love with Anne,' explained Mary stiffly. 'And in 1533 when I was seventeen he had his marriage to Mummy annulled, which I expect Anne told you. Then Mummy was sent to a castle in Cambridgeshire and I had to go and live with my baby sister, Elizabeth, who was Anne's daughter in Hatfield.'

'You poor thing,' said Phoebe with sympathy. 'That must have been horrible.'

'It was.' Mary started walking along the river bank, Phoebe following at her side. 'I wasn't allowed to see Mummy again, and my place in the line to the throne was taken by Elizabeth.'

'Why?' asked Phoebe.

'Because I was a Catholic and Daddy had formed his own Protestant church to marry Anne. He said that because I wouldn't give up my religion and because his marriage to Mummy was illegal, I didn't have any legal right to be Queen.'

Phoebe stopped in horror and bent down to pick up a pebble. Hurling it into the river, she was rewarded with the sound of a very loud splash.

'What's wrong?' Mary demanded. 'Girls don't throw dirty great rocks into the river!'

'I do!' replied Phoebe firmly. 'And your dad was a big bully! I haven't heard one nice thing about him yet.'

'I guess he wasn't very nice,' sighed Mary. 'I mean, at first he was nice to me. When I was little he cuddled and played with me. I was the apple of his eye. But when Daddy met Anne he had no room for me and Mummy anymore.'

'So what happened next?' asked Phoebe, her arm aching after hurling the pebble so hard.

'Well, I refused to talk to Anne or Daddy. I wouldn't accept Anne as Queen and I didn't recognise Elizabeth as a princess either,' Mary admitted.

'I bet your dad didn't like that.'

'Not much.' Mary smiled. 'We didn't talk to each

other for three years. And then when Mummy died in 1536, I was all alone.'

Phoebe's heart went out to Mary. Her new guide might be a bit full of herself but she didn't deserve to be lonely. As she linked her arm through Mary's she suddenly felt the earth shudder. Looking down at her feet, Phoebe was astonished to see dirt flying everywhere and the trees swoosh unnervingly.

'What's going on?' Phoebe cried.

'I'm trying to get us to the next place!' Mary said, screwing up her eyes in frustration. 'I told you I haven't really mastered this flying thing yet.'

Just then the ground disappeared from beneath them and Phoebe and Mary shot into the air.

CHAPTER TEN

Mary guided them further out of the city. Higher and higher they flew, passing field after field and town after town, until finally they landed with an almighty bump, inside a very long hall.

Dusting herself down, Phoebe took a deep breath and tried to settle her tummy. Flying with Mary was worse than being on an aeroplane with really bad turbulence!

Looking around her, Phoebe saw the hall had long wooden beams and high windows. As Phoebe got to her feet, her tummy let out a very large rumble.

'It's not my fault! I haven't eaten all day,' Phoebe

apologised.

'You mean nobody's fed you?' Mary gasped.

Phoebe shook her head.

Mary clapped her hands. Instantly a young girl dressed simply in a brown dress, a white head scarf and apron appeared, and curtseyed.

'We'd like some food,' Mary snapped and the girl dipped her head and hurried away.

Within minutes, she reappeared bearing so much food the poor girl struggled to carry it.

'Set it down over there,' Mary instructed, pointing to a large wooden table in the middle of the room.

Phoebe's mouth watered. There were lots of different meats, bread, vegetables and even a small fruit tart with custard.

As Mary sat down, she reached for a leg of pork

and took a massive bite. Phoebe did just the same.

'So why are we here?' Phoebe asked, trying not to talk with her mouth full.

'This is Hatfield House,' Mary explained. 'I lived here after Mummy died and Daddy had Anne beheaded so he could marry Jane Seymour. Jane was lovely and helped me and Daddy make up.'

'Gosh! Did he put you in line for the throne again?' Phoebe asked.

Mary shook her head. 'No. He made me accept I had no claim to the throne and he was the rightful head of the Church of England, otherwise known as the Protestants. But as a Catholic that was very hard for me to do.'

'So what *did* you do?' Phoebe asked, gnawing another piece of pork.

'I said I accepted it, but I didn't really,' Mary explained. 'Anyway, Daddy seemed happy enough so he arranged for me to live here and gave me lots of money for nice clothes to wear.'

'Oooh, show me,' begged Phoebe, who was desperate for a peek inside Mary's wardrobe.

'Alright!' Mary smiled, leading Phoebe along the corridor and into another high-beamed room filled with gown after gown.

'Are these all yours?' Phoebe gasped as she rushed over to the rack of gorgeous dresses, petticoats and bodices.

'Well, we couldn't have the King's daughter wearing any old thing, could we? After Jane died in 1537 giving birth to my little brother, Edward, Daddy made me his godmother,' Mary told Phoebe.

'And did you all live happily ever after?' Phoebe asked, stroking the sleeve of one of the dresses.

'Not really, no,' said Mary with a sigh. 'Daddy married a lady named Anne of Cleeves but then decided he didn't like her so that marriage was annulled. Then he married another lady called Catherine Howard and had her beheaded too.'

'I wonder why your dad got married so often when he always tried to get out of being married,' Phoebe pondered.

'I've often wondered that myself,' Mary muttered dryly. 'Anyway, then Daddy married his sixth and final wife, Catherine Parr, who convinced Daddy I should be allowed to take the throne after Edward.'

'That was nice,' Phoebe smiled.

'Catherine *was* nice,' said Mary. She beamed as she

said it. 'Thanks to her, Daddy and I were on very good terms when he died in 1547. That was when Edward, who had been raised as a Protestant, became King.'

'What happened to you?' Phoebe asked.

'Well, I was still Catholic so Edward and I fought like cat and dog over religion.'

'That seems silly,' said Phoebe. 'Now there are lots of different religions and you can worship who you want.'

'It wasn't always like that,' Mary said. 'Eddie wanted me to abandon Catholicism but I refused. Then when he died in 1553, and I took over the throne from Jane, I was so popular with my subjects that I abolished the Bibles Eddie put in the churches and put all the Catholic ones back.'

'Wow! You were busy,' Phoebe marvelled. 'Did

you have help?'

'My husband, Prince Philip of Spain, was also a Catholic, so he helped a bit,' Mary said bashfully.

'Husband!' Phoebe shrieked excitedly. 'Why didn't you tell me about him before? What was he like?'

'He was lovely. Tall, dark hair and a beautiful Spanish accent,' Mary said, pointing to a portrait hanging on the wall. 'That's him there.'

'He is gorgeous,' Phoebe agreed.

'I thought so,' Mary sighed. 'I was sent that portrait before I met him. As soon as I saw it I fell in love.'

CHAPTER ELEVEN

Mary gripped Phoebe's hand. As they flew at breakneck speed, this time the little girl had a strong sense of where they were going. They landed in the grounds of what Phoebe knew was Winchester Cathedral.

'We got married here in 1554,' explained Mary. 'Philip couldn't speak a word of English so the ceremony was a mixture of Spanish, French and Latin.'

'Lucky you learned all those languages when you were little,' Phoebe said.

'Exactly!' Mary agreed as they wandered arm in arm towards the cathedral's altar. 'I've always said a good education can do wonders for a girl's love life.'

'Did you have any babies?' Phoebe asked.

Mary shook her head, sadness crossing her face. 'Sadly Philip and I weren't blessed with babies so instead we concentrated on making everyone Catholic.'

'Weren't the Protestants upset you were trying to get them to change their religion?' Phoebe demanded.

'Yes,' Mary explained impatiently. 'But their religion was made up by Daddy. So I said if they believed in a different religion from me, then I would see it as an act of defiance and they would suffer.'

Phoebe's eyes widened with fear. 'So what did you do to the Protestants?'

Mary giggled. 'I burnt three hundred of them!'

'You what?!' Shocked, Phoebe backed away from Mary and threw herself onto the nearest pew.

'They deserved it,' said Mary with a shrug. 'If they couldn't recognise Catholicism was the only religion to practice, they had to die.'

'But how could you do that?' Phoebe asked, bewildered. 'You knew how awful it was yourself when you couldn't be openly Catholic because your dad created the Church of England.'

'I tried to get people to see reason and they wouldn't,' Mary said with a hiss. 'They brought it on themselves.'

'I bet everyone hated you for it!' said Phoebe defiantly.

Mary shuffled her feet uncomfortably. 'It's true I wasn't very popular with my subjects. They nicknamed me Bloody Mary.'

'So that's where that comes from!' Phoebe gasped.

'I thought it was just a drink Mummy likes after she's had a long day meeting people. Well, you deserved to be called bad names if you killed people just because their religion was different to yours.'

'I don't care,' Mary said, squaring her shoulders. 'It's a tough job being Queen, as you'll find out for yourself one day.'

'I know I'll never kill anyone for believing something differently to me!' Phoebe huffed.

'Well said, Phoebe,' came a voice from just behind her.

Spinning around, Phoebe saw a woman with flaming red hair and pale white skin walking towards her.

'Elizabeth!' Mary hissed. 'What are you doing here?'

'You've had your time with our young friend.'

Elizabeth smiled. 'It's my turn now.'

'Wait. Who are you?' Phoebe demanded.

'This is my half-sister, Elizabeth I,' Mary explained.

'She always did have a talent for turning up where

she wasn't wanted.'

'Oh wow,' Phoebe said, getting to her feet and

walking towards the smiling Elizabeth. 'I've heard a lot about you.'

'Then we'll have great fun together as I tell you my story.' Elizabeth said, clapping her hands in delight. 'Let's go.'

Phoebe was about to slide her hand into Elizabeth's when she stopped. 'Wait. I haven't heard the rest of Mary's story.'

Elizabeth yawned. 'It's very dull. Nobody liked her after she killed loads of Protestants and Philip never really loved her, he just fancied the idea of being a king. When Mary didn't produce any children he left her on her own a lot because Spain and England were fighting against France.'

'Philip loved me!' Mary protested.

'If you say so,' Elizabeth said with a smirk. 'But he

asked me to marry him the moment you died in 1558 and I became Queen.'

Phoebe's head was spinning. She turned to Mary. 'Wait. You died?'

Mary nodded. 'Yes. I was forty-two and I'd been ill for a while. Nobody really knew what was wrong with me then, but now I would have been diagnosed with cancer.'

'I'm sorry,' Phoebe whispered.

Mary didn't seem to hear her. 'I had hoped Elizabeth would carry on the work I'd started, returning Catholicism to the country, but she let me down.'

'Did not,' Elizabeth fired back.

'Did so.' Mary glowered. 'You sided with Daddy and made England Protestant again.'

'Mary, do you fight with everyone you meet?' Phoebe said, interrupting the two sisters.

Elizabeth laughed. 'With a nickname like Bloody Mary, you can say that again.'

'Well, it isn't very nice,' Phoebe said to Mary before turning to Elizabeth. 'And as for you, you shouldn't be so mean to your sister.'

'Oh don't be such a spoilsport,' said Elizabeth with a giggle. 'Come on – now you've heard all about boring Bloody Mary it's time for some fun.'

Without waiting for an answer, Elizabeth reached for Phoebe's hand and whisked Phoebe into the air, leaving the young princess with just enough time to shout goodbye to Mary.

CHAPTER TWELVE

'Where are we going?' cried Phoebe as she spun around in dizzying circles. They'd been flying for a good ten minutes and Phoebe wondered if they'd ever get down.

'I haven't done this for ages,' Elizabeth giggled. 'Come on, Phoebe, live a little.'

With that, Elizabeth twirled Phoebe upside down, before bringing her gently to the ground. Phoebe had spent so much time flying upside down she wondered if she should apply to be in the Red Arrows!

'Westminster Abbey,' said Phoebe in awe.

'Certainly is,' replied Elizabeth as she dusted off

her dress. 'This is where I was crowned Queen in 1559 after Mary popped her clogs.'

'But what about your early life?' Phoebe asked. So far, all the other princesses had started their stories by telling Phoebe how their lives began – Elizabeth had jumped straight to the good bit.

'What about it?' Elizabeth said with a shrug. 'Didn't the others tell you everything?'

Phoebe's confused face said it all, so Elizabeth flopped onto a nearby pew.

'Fine,' she said with a sigh. 'In a nutshell, I was born at Greenwich Palace on the 7th September 1533. My mum was Anne Boleyn, dad was Henry VIII.

'Dad had Mum's head chopped off when I was nearly three and I was brought up by lots of different mistresses, until eventually Dad and I made up thanks to his wife Catherine, and my place in line to the throne was restored. Then, just before stupid old Mary died, she had the good sense to name me the next Queen.'

'Why wouldn't she have done?' asked Phoebe. 'She was your sister.'

'Pah! You'd never know it!' grumbled Elizabeth. 'That woman locked me up in the Tower of London and was going to have me beheaded. She had convinced herself that I was trying to become Queen myself. All because I was a Protestant and she was a Catholic.'

'Not the religion again!' moaned Phoebe. 'Seriously this is getting really old.'

'You're telling me,' Elizabeth said with a sniff. 'Anyway, I was so brilliant and clever at arguing, I persuaded her that she was wrong. Finally she agreed that I could be Queen. Let me tell you, it was the best Coronation ever!'

'What do you mean?' asked Phoebe, as she followed Elizabeth inside the cathedral.

'Well, I wasn't just going to settle for any old ceremony, Phoebe,' Elizabeth exclaimed.

'What did you do?' Phoebe asked, already dreading the answer. Despite only spending less than half an hour with Elizabeth, Phoebe had a feeling that Elizabeth didn't do things by halves.

'First of all, I wore this beautiful gown, as you can see here.' Elizabeth smiled, pointing to a portrait on the wall.

Phoebe peered at the picture. There was no denying it; Elizabeth looked gorgeous in the gold gown.

'Wasn't I brilliant?' asked Elizabeth. She was

laughing and clapping her hands in glee! Without waiting for an answer, Elizabeth continued to pace theatrically up and down the abbey aisle.

'I arranged for the streets of London to be lined with blue cloth to celebrate my Coronation,' Elizabeth continued. 'Afterwards everybody ripped the cloth to shreds so they each had a souvenir. Then I got a friend of mine, a mathematician called John Dee, to work out the best date and time for me to be crowned.'

'How does that work?' Phoebe demanded. 'Mummy says that being crowned should happen as quickly as possible.'

'Well yes, obviously,' groaned Elizabeth. 'But if you can't be made Queen at a time that suits you, then, honestly, Phoebe, what on earth is the point of being a queen at all?'

Elizabeth walked towards the stage of the abbey and flung herself onto the nearby throne.

'Anyway, I got my friend John to work out my birth chart. He looked at the stars, moon and sun and aligned it with the time I was born. Then he worked out when I should be made Queen,' Elizabeth explained.

'What if he got it wrong?' Phoebe asked, as she sat in a pew opposite Elizabeth.

'He wouldn't. Besides, if he had I would have had his head cut off,' Elizabeth laughed.

'You are joking?' Phoebe asked gobsmacked. 'You'd kill someone for one tiny mistake?'

'Maybe!' Elizabeth smirked, before getting up from her throne and walking across the stage towards Phoebe. 'And I thought Mary was serious! You need to lighten up, Phoebe. Being Queen is fun.'

Elizabeth grabbed Phoebe's hand and whisked her outside the abbey. A large crowd had gathered to celebrate the new Queen Elizabeth.

'See!' shouted Elizabeth above the noise. 'Everyone loved me.'

The noise of organs, pipes, trumpets, drums and, of course, cheers were so loud Phoebe had to put her hands over her ears. 'Can we go back inside?' she shouted. 'I can't hear you.'

'What's that?' asked Elizabeth, who was so into the party spirit that she was being hoisted onto the shoulders of several of her subjects.

Phoebe didn't know whether to laugh or cry at the sight of one of the most famous women in the world cheering at the top of her voice. 'Come on, Phoebe,' Elizabeth called. 'Join the party.'

With that Phoebe too was hoisted onto the shoulders of the crowd. As the whoops and cheers became louder, Phoebe couldn't stop laughing. This was one of the maddest situations she'd ever found herself in.

'Told you!' Elizabeth shouted above the din. 'As Queen you've got to live a little. And not only that, you've got to remember to look after your subjects.'

'What do you mean?' Phoebe shouted.

'What?' Elizabeth called.

'I said, what do you mean?' Phoebe tried again.

But Elizabeth shook her head. 'It's no good. I can't hear a word you're saying. Hang on.'

Suddenly Phoebe felt Elizabeth slip her hand into hers, and in the blink of an eye she was standing outside a huge palace in the centre of London. Phoebe had to hand it to Elizabeth; she was a lot better at flying than any of her friends.

CHAPTER THIRTEEN

'What is this place?' Phoebe asked.

'Whitehall Palace, silly,' Elizabeth replied as she led Phoebe inside. 'It's the largest palace in the whole of Europe, and the centre of government.'

'Wow,' Phoebe marvelled as she took in the ornate architecture, indoor tennis court, bowling green and jousting yard.

'Daddy had all of those put in,' Elizabeth said, waving her hands dismissively. 'He loved to have a good time.'

'Did you and your dad make up then?' Phoebe asked, struggling to keep up with Elizabeth as she strode through the palace.

'Oh, Daddy was just Daddy.' She shrugged. 'I loved him, and he loved me in his own way.'

'But he beheaded your mum!' Phoebe exclaimed so loudly that Elizabeth stopped in the middle of the courtyard and pulled her to one side.

'Ssssh!' she hissed. 'All this talk of beheading makes people nervous. Look, it was all a long time ago. You've got to forgive and forget.'

'But wasn't it hard growing up without a mummy? If my daddy ever did anything horrible to my mum, I'd never forgive him.'

'Well, we're all different, aren't we?' Elizabeth said. 'At the end of the day, Daddy and I had a lot in common, and not just the red hair! We loved poetry and languages. Daddy and I also spoke Latin, French and Italian, and we both shared ideas about the way to run the country.'

'Like what?!' Phoebe demanded.

'Like helping poor people have a better life. I made laws that gave poor people and their children a chance to work or learn a new skill. I set up hospitals and orphanages for poor people who were too young, too old or too sick to go to work.'

'That's nice,' said Phoebe with a smile. So far, she'd thought Elizabeth was a lot of fun but a bit selfish. It was nice to hear she'd put a lot of people first.

'Well, it was,' giggled Elizabeth. 'But if people were too idle to go to work and pretended they were poorly, I put them in prison!'

'Prison!' squeaked Phoebe. 'That seems a bit harsh.'

'That's the thing about being a queen, Phoebe.

Sometimes you have to be harsh and sometimes you get to have lots of fun.' Elizabeth smiled.

As Elizabeth reached for Phoebe's hand, she noticed the ground swayed a bit to the left, then to the right, and suddenly they were up high up in the air without a hint of wooshiness in Phoebe's tummy.

'You're really good at this,' said Phoebe, marvelling as they flew across the city.

'I know!' laughed Elizabeth.

Within minutes they'd landed at a landmark Phoebe knew well.

'This is Shakespeare's Globe, isn't it?' Phoebe said. 'Mummy takes me to see lots of very boring plays here.'

'They're not boring!' Elizabeth exclaimed as she led Phoebe into the heart of the theatre. 'In fact, when you're Queen you get to have so much fun you can even make friends with authors and playwrights and

get them to

write things

for you.'

'Is that what

you did?' Phoebe

asked. Elizabeth

nodded smugly.

'I loved the theatre.

I even started my own

acting company called the Queen's Men.

'William Shakespeare was part of this, you know.

He even made a reference to me in his very famous

play *A Midsummer Night's Dream*.'

By now Phoebe was agog. Sat cross-legged on the

floor, she watched transfixed as Elizabeth took to the

stage.

'A fair vestal throned by the west,' Elizabeth boomed.

Clapping her hands together to give Elizabeth a round of applause, Phoebe got to her feet.

'Wow! Shakespeare really wrote that for you?' she asked. 'You're so lucky a man liked you so much he wrote a play for you.'

Beaming, Elizabeth got off the stage and sat on one of the chairs.

'He did like me, but not in a romantic way, Phoebe,' Elizabeth explained. 'He liked me because I was interested in plays and the theatre.'

'Oh.' Phoebe looked disappointed. Elizabeth was so pretty it would have been nice if William Shakespeare had been her boyfriend.

'So who was your husband then?' Phoebe asked.

'I never had one,' Elizabeth replied simply.

'What!' Phoebe cried aghast. 'Aren't all princesses and queens meant to fall in love and have lots of babies?'

'Well, some do,' explained Elizabeth carefully. 'But the most important thing for a princess or queen to do is to look after their people. I mean, I had a few potential boyfriends but nothing came of it.'

'Who?' demanded Phoebe, desperate to hear some gossip.

'Let's see, there was Robert Dudley but he was just a friend. Then there was Sir Walter Raleigh but he too was just a friend, and then of course there was my great pal Sir Francis Drake, who helped defeat the Spanish Armada in 1588. I knighted him as a thank you,' Elizabeth explained.

'But why didn't you marry any of them?' Phoebe asked.

'Because there's more to life than marrying boys!' Elizabeth hissed. 'I'll have you know I was too busy protecting our country and my life.'

'Did you go to war then?' Phoebe asked, hastily
changing the subject.

'Yes, with the Spanish. In 1588 the Spanish sent an
awful lot of ships to England to try to start a war but,

of course, we defeated them,' Elizabeth explained.

'How?' Phoebe asked.

Getting to her feet, Elizabeth walked back across the stage. 'We set fire to a lot of the ships,' she explained. 'And I gave this brilliant speech that all the troops loved. Look, I'll do it for you now.'

Clearing her throat, Elizabeth stood in the centre of the stage and looked at Phoebe.

'I know I have the body but of a weak and feeble woman, but I have the heart and stomach of a king and of a King of England too,' Elizabeth boomed.

'Bravo!' applauded Phoebe. 'That was really good.'

'Thank you,' said Elizabeth, smiling and taking a small bow.

'But I'm a bit confused. Where I come from women are just as good as men. Mummy's always telling

Daddy that without her he'd be useless. Does that mean women weren't equal when you were Queen?' Phoebe asked.

Elizabeth sat back on the stage and shook her head. 'Sadly not. Everyone was more worried about my love life and producing an heir to the throne than how I ran the country! It wasn't until I gave *that* speech that I was taken seriously.'

'It was a really good speech,' Phoebe chimed. 'But wait a minute. You said something about protecting your life. Who tried to kill you?'

'You'll never believe it, Phoebe, but not everyone was happy about me being Queen,' Elizabeth began. 'The Catholics in the country didn't want me because I was a Protestant.'

'Oh no!' Phoebe grumbled. 'Not the religious stuff

again.'

'Yes, the religious stuff again,' Elizabeth said, rather annoyed. 'Mary Queen of Scots thought she should be Queen of England as well, so together with all her Catholic friends she came up with a plot to kill me.'

'How horrible,' Phoebe gasped. 'Were you frightened?'

'I certainly was not!' Elizabeth exclaimed. 'Fortunately I had some wonderful friends like Sir Francis Walsingham, who was my secretary of state. He discovered the plot and suggested we make a law called the Bond of Association.'

'Sounds like a film,' Phoebe marvelled. 'What did that mean?'

'It meant that anyone who plotted to assassinate me or tried to rule England in my place would be killed.'

'I said it before and I'll say it again, that seems a bit harsh,' said Phoebe.

'They were trying to kill me!' shrieked Elizabeth. 'It was no more than they deserved.'

'So what happened next?' asked Phoebe quickly.

'Francis found out that Mary and all her Catholic pals had been writing coded letters and were planning to have me bumped off. With this evidence, what else could we do?' said Elizabeth with a shrug.

'Kill them?' Phoebe asked.

'I had to. They'd broken the law,' Elizabeth pointed out. 'I must admit it was hard to sign the death warrant of my own cousin though. Nobody wants to murder someone they're related to – well, apart from Daddy maybe!'

Phoebe chuckled. 'What happened then? You had

no family of your own.'

'My country was my family, Phoebe.' Elizabeth explained, reaching for the little girl's hand. 'It was a huge honour and privilege to serve my country. I hope you remember that when you're Queen someday.'

CHAPTER FOURTEEN

The ground shook very slightly and Phoebe realised they'd landed back at Westminster Abbey and she'd barely noticed.

'What are we doing here again?' Phoebe asked.

'I wanted to show you my place of rest,' Elizabeth explained, walking over towards her tomb. I died in 1603 aged sixty-nine. Because I had no heir, I named James VI of Scotland my successor.'

'Oh, you're buried with Mary,' Phoebe exclaimed as she examined Elizabeth's coffin.

'Yes. We are sisters after all. It's only right we spend eternity together. Even though, between you and me, Phoebe, she is very boring!'

'I heard that!' a voice called.

Swinging around, Phoebe saw Mary had joined them. Anne and Jane were also there.

'What are you doing here?' Phoebe gasped.

'We wanted to say goodbye together,' Anne explained. 'Our time with you is up.'

'No!' wailed Phoebe. 'I want to stay a bit longer.'

But Mary shook her head. 'I'm sorry, but you have to go now. We hope our stories will assist you in becoming a good princess and queen.'

Phoebe felt her eyes well up with tears. She didn't

want to say goodbye to her new friends.

Phoebe turned to Jane. 'I now understand that there's more to being a queen than just pretty clothes,' she whispered. She took Anne's hand. 'I will try my hardest to always be nice and not let the bullies get me down.' She smiled at Mary. 'I now appreciate how valuable an education is.' Finally she turned to Elizabeth. 'It doesn't matter if you're a man or a woman as long as you do your best. That's all anyone can ask of you.'

As Phoebe finished, Anne, Mary, Elizabeth and Jane smiled at one another.

'I think we've taught you everything we know,' Anne grinned.

'Time to put it all into practice,' added Elizabeth.

As Mary, Jane, Elizabeth and Anne all waved

goodbye, Phoebe felt the ground beneath her start to shake and the familiar wooshy sensation in her tummy return.

'Bye!' Phoebe shouted as she rose higher and higher into the air. 'It was nice to meet you all!'

EPILOGUE

As Phoebe hurtled back to the ground with a bump, she was amazed to see she was back in her mum's closet and surrounded by mess. Quickly Phoebe sprang into action and started shoving shoes into boxes and clothes into wardrobes, when suddenly she heard her mum calling. Despite her best efforts to tidy up there were still heaps of her mum's dresses, bracelets and shoes everywhere.

'Phoebe!' Queen Alice hollered. 'It's dinner time.'

'Coming,' Phoebe called, as her mum popped her head around the door.

'I've been calling you for the last ten minutes!' Alice

exclaimed. 'What have you been doing?'

'Erm, I fell asleep. I was tired, Mummy,' Phoebe lied.

'I'm not surprised!' Alice grumbled. 'You wore yourself out making all this mess. You'll have to finish tidying after dinner. Come on.'

As Phoebe followed her mum down the stairs and into the huge banqueting room, she blearily rubbed her eyes. Had meeting Anne, Mary, Elizabeth and Jane all been a huge dream? It didn't seem like it at the time. But now, as she tucked into her huge plate of spaghetti Bolognese and listened to her little brother go on and on about scoring a goal at school, the whole thing seemed a bit far-fetched.

'And what about you, Phoebe?' Alice asked, interrupting her daydreams. 'What did you do at school today?'

'Maths!' Phoebe moaned. 'My worst subject.'

'Everyone knows girls are rubbish at maths!' Peter laughed.

'Are not!' Phoebe told him.

'Are too,' Peter insisted.

'Don't be such a fopdoodle,' Phoebe hissed.

'Mum! Phoebe just said a bad word,' Peter insisted.

'No I didn't!' Phoebe exclaimed. 'It's another word for idiot.'

Queen Alice thumped the table in exasperation. 'That's enough, both of you! If you can't behave at the dinner table, then you don't get to eat your dinner. Peter, go to your room, and, Phoebe, clean that mess up.'

'Yes, Mum,' Phoebe groaned as she got up from

the dinner table and followed her little brother up the stairs.

Opening the door to her mum's room, Phoebe's heart sank. There was so much to put away. Still, she realised as she folded, sorted, and straightened the clothes she'd been playing with, there was no point moaning about it.

Spotting the photo album in the corner, Phoebe started flicking through the pages once more. There was Princess Paula with the wonky nose, and of course Lady Louise with the cauliflower ears.

Turning the page to see Anne Boleyn, Phoebe ran her fingers over the image just as her mum walked into the room holding a plate of spaghetti.

'Thought you might be hungry,' Alice smiled, setting the plate down. 'Cleaning up and time travelling with Anne Boleyn and her friends always used to make me tired when I was your age.'

Phoebe gasped at her mum in amazement. 'You met them too?'

'I did,' Alice grinned. 'I was about your age, and I had great fun with Elizabeth, Anne, Mary and Jane Grey. I never wanted to go home, they were such a giggle.'

'I thought I'd dreamt it.'

'You didn't,' said Alice, sitting next to Phoebe on the floor and putting the plate in the middle of them. 'But when I saw the photo album opened at Anne's picture, and you were nowhere to be found, I knew where you were.'

'It felt like I'd been gone ages,' Phoebe said.

'Always does,' Alice agreed.

'You've seen them more than once?' Phoebe gasped. 'How long did you have to wait? Can I see them again tomorrow?'

Alice threw her head back and laughed. 'If only it were that simple. I've seen them three times, and I know Anne, Mary, Elizabeth and Jane will have shared with you some very valuable lessons, but let me teach you one – patience. You'll see them again, but it will be when you least expect it.'

Getting up from the floor, Alice crossed the room and opened the door. 'Don't stay up too late tidying.' She grinned.

As Alice shut the door, Phoebe looked at the photo of Anne once more.

Then, without warning, the picture started to move. First it juddered to the left. Then to the right, and just as before, Anne's hand came to life and it reached out

from the photo towards Phoebe.

'See you again soon, Phoebe,' Anne said. 'We've

a lot more stories to share.'